ASTERIX THE GAUL

TEXT BY GOSCINNY

DRAWINGS BY UDERZO

TRANSLATED BY ANTHEA BELL AND DEREK HOCKRIDGE

HODDER DARGAUD
LONDON SYDNEY AUCKLAND

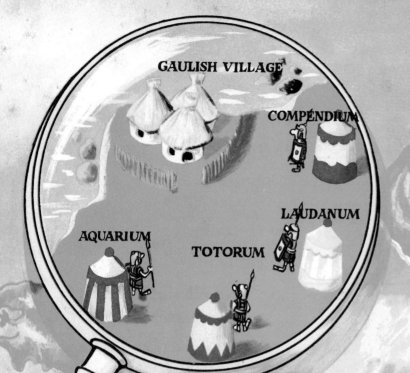

GAULISH VILLAGE

COMPENDIUM

LAUDANUM

AQUARIUM

TOTORUM

ARMORICA

BELGICA

LUTETIA

SPQR

GAUL
(ROMAN CONQUEST)
50 B.C.

CELTICA

AQUITANIA

PROVINCIA

The year is 50 BC. Gaul is entirely occupied by the Romans.
Well, not entirely . . . One small village of indomitable Gauls still
holds out against the invaders. And life is not easy for the
Roman legionaries who garrison the fortified camps of
Totorum, Aquarium, Laudanum and Compendium . . .

a few of the Gauls

Asterix, the hero of these adventures. A shrewd, cunning little warrior; all perilous missions are immediately entrusted to him. Asterix gets his superhuman strength from the magic potion brewed by the druid Getafix…

Obelix, Asterix's inseparable friend. A menhir delivery-man by trade; addicted to wild boar. Obelix is always ready to drop everything and go off on a new adventure with Asterix – so long as there's wild boar to eat, and plenty of fighting.

Getafix, the venerable village druid. Gathers mistletoe and brews magic potions. His speciality is the potion which gives the drinker superhuman strength. But Getafix also has other recipes up his sleeve…

Cacofonix, the bard. Opinion is divided as to his musical gifts. Cacofonix thinks he's a genius. Everyone else thinks he's un-speakable. But so long as he doesn't speak, let alone sing, everybody likes him…

Finally, Vitalstatistix, the chief of the tribe. Majestic, brave and hot-tempered, the old warrior is respected by his men and feared by his enemies. Vitalstatistix himself has only one fear; he is afraid the sky may fall on his head tomorrow. But as he always says, 'Tomorrow never comes.'

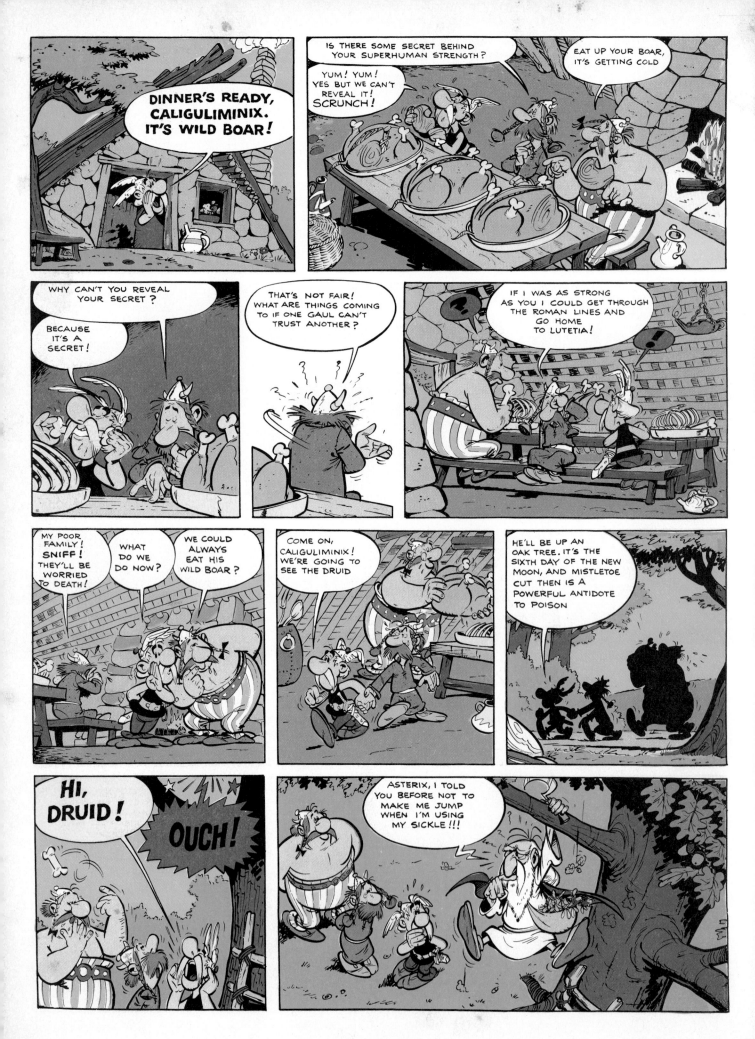

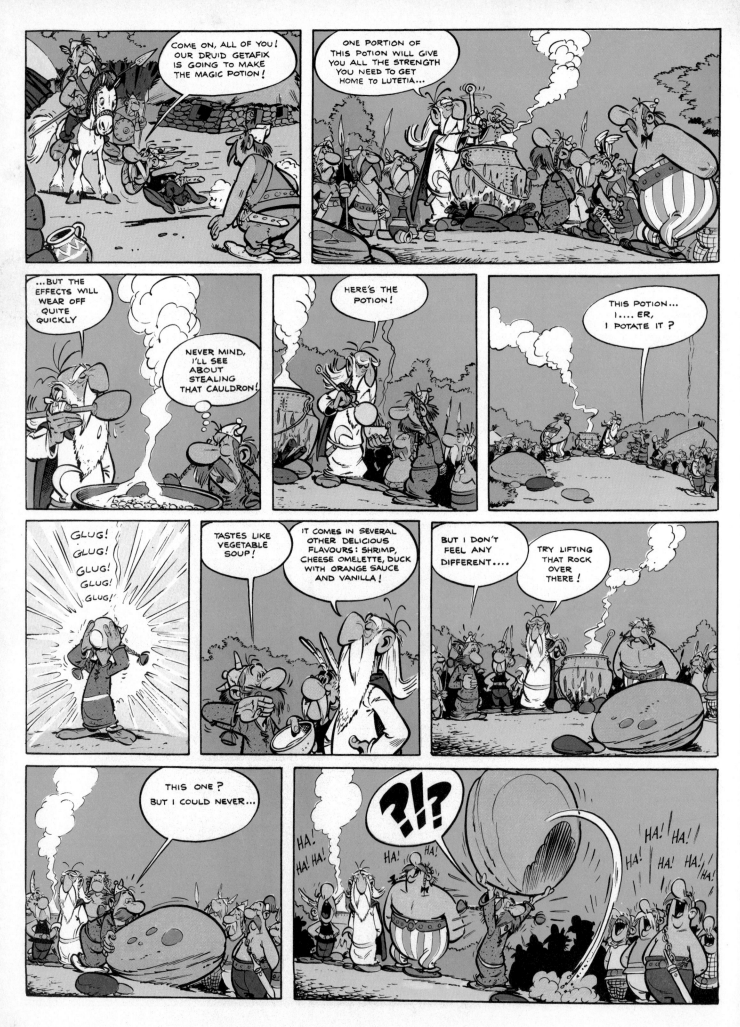

22

23

24

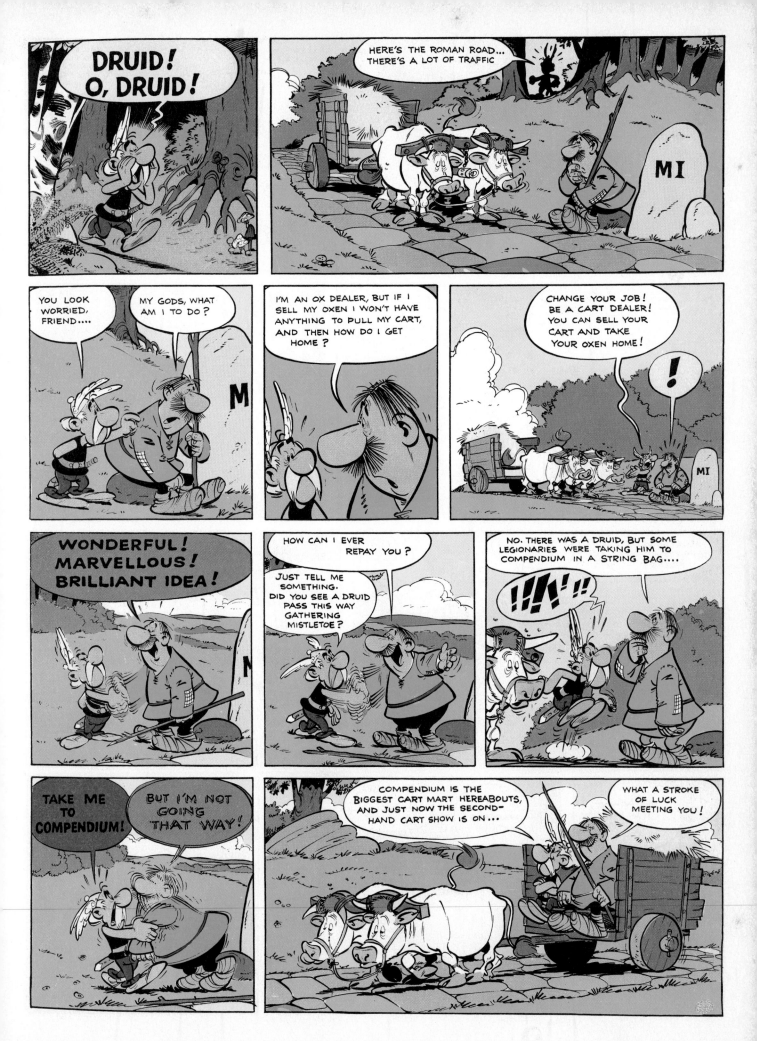

40

41

43

45

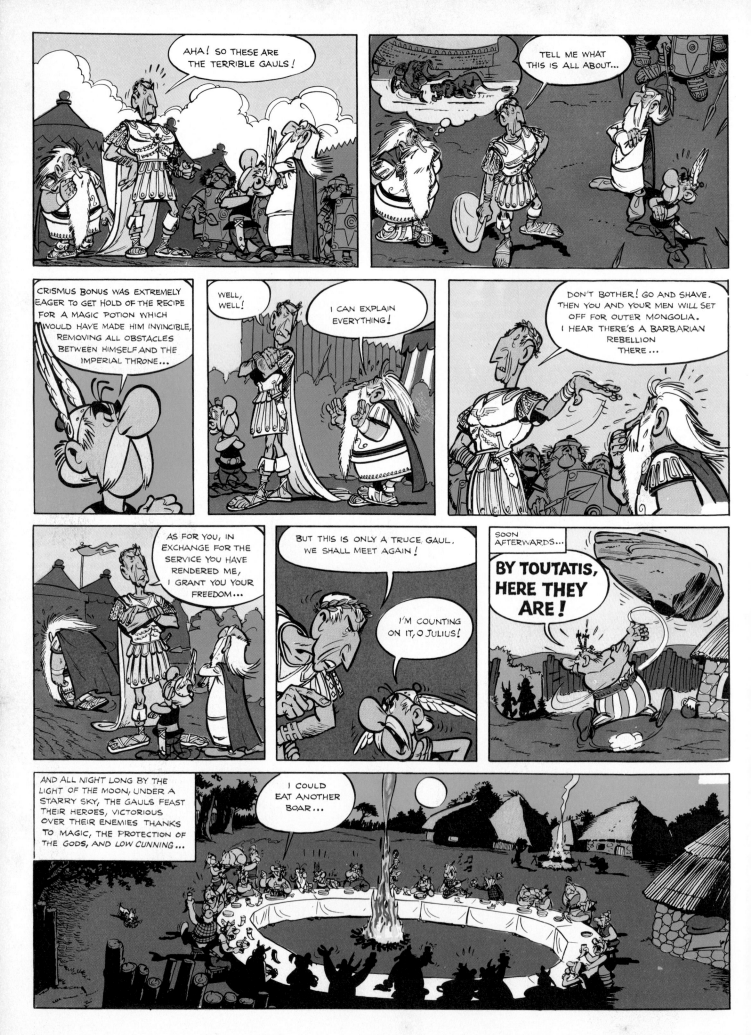

ASTERIX IN SPAIN

TEXT BY GOSCINNY

DRAWINGS BY UDERZO

TRANSLATED BY ANTHEA BELL AND DEREK HOCKRIDGE

GAULISH VILLAGE

COMPENDIUM

LAUDANUM

AQUARIUM

TOTORUM

ARMORICA

BELGICA

LUTETIA

SPQR

GAUL
(ROMAN CONQUEST)
50 B.C.

CELTICA

PROVINCIA

AQUITANIA

The year is 50 BC. Gaul is entirely occupied by the Romans. Well, not entirely… One small village of indomitable Gauls still holds out against the invaders. And life is not easy for the Roman legionaries who garrison the fortified camps of Totorum, Aquarium, Laudanum and Compendium…

a few of the Gauls

Asterix, the hero of these adventures. A shrewd, cunning little warrior; all perilous missions are immediately entrusted to him. Asterix gets his superhuman strength from the magic potion brewed by the druid Getafix...

Obelix, Asterix's inseparable friend. A menhir delivery-man by trade; addicted to wild boar. Obelix is always ready to drop everything and go off on a new adventure with Asterix – so long as there's wild boar to eat, and plenty of fighting.

Getafix, the venerable village druid. Gathers mistletoe and brews magic potions. His speciality is the potion which gives the drinker superhuman strength. But Getafix also has other recipes up his sleeve...

Cacofonix, the bard. Opinion is divided as to his musical gifts. Cacofonix thinks he's a genius. Everyone else thinks he's un-speakable. But so long as he doesn't speak, let alone sing, everybody likes him...

Finally, Vitalstatistix, the chief of the tribe. Majestic, brave and hot-tempered, the old warrior is respected by his men and feared by his enemies. Vitalstatistix himself has only one fear; he is afraid the sky may fall on his head tomorrow. But as he always says, 'Tomorrow never comes.'

7

11

13

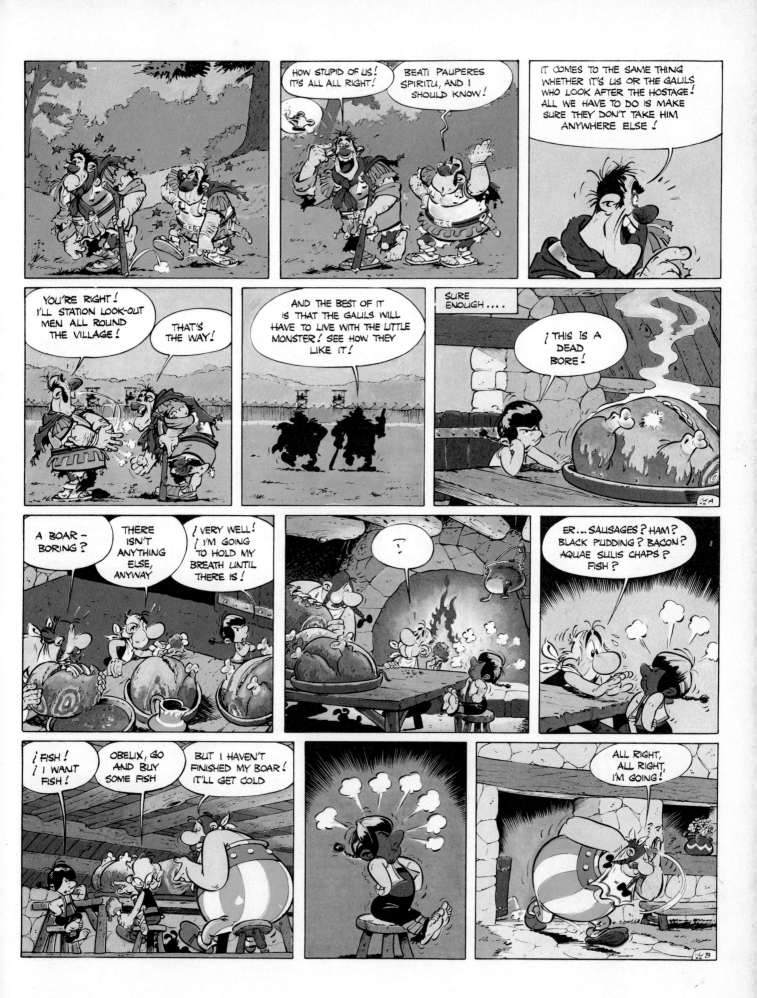

15

16

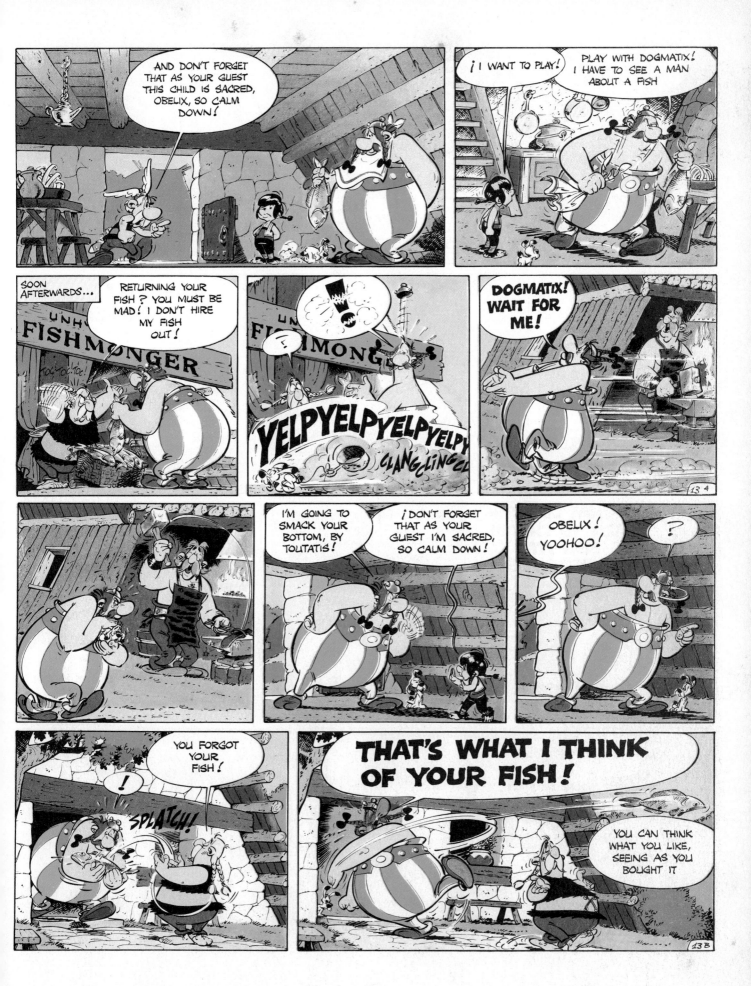

19

20

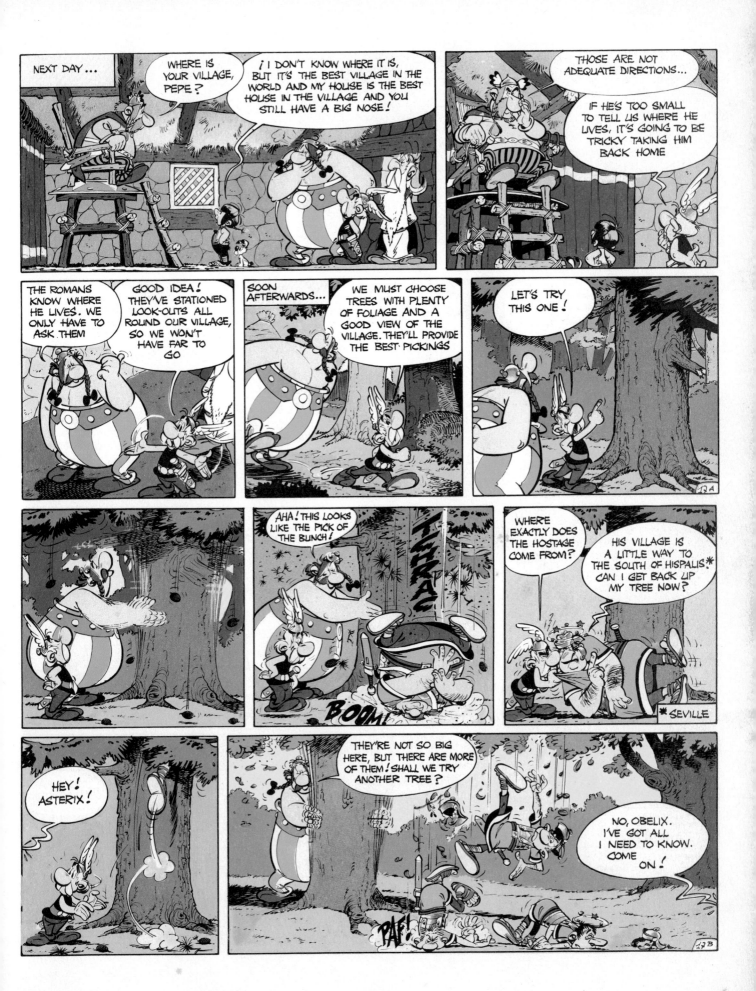

21

22

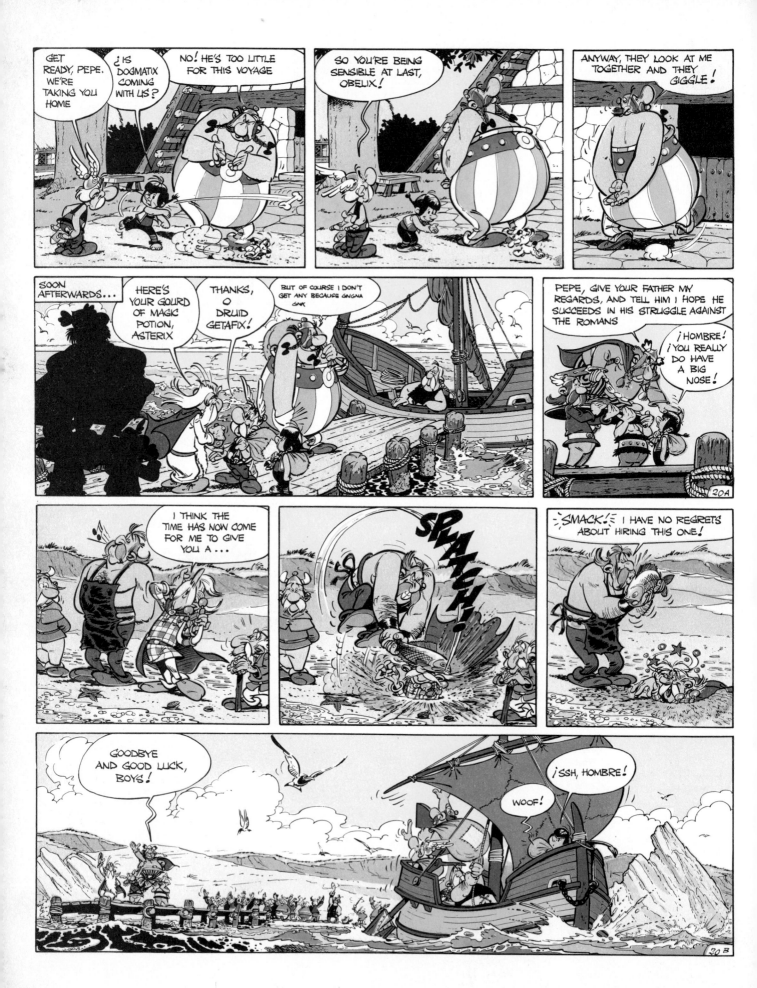

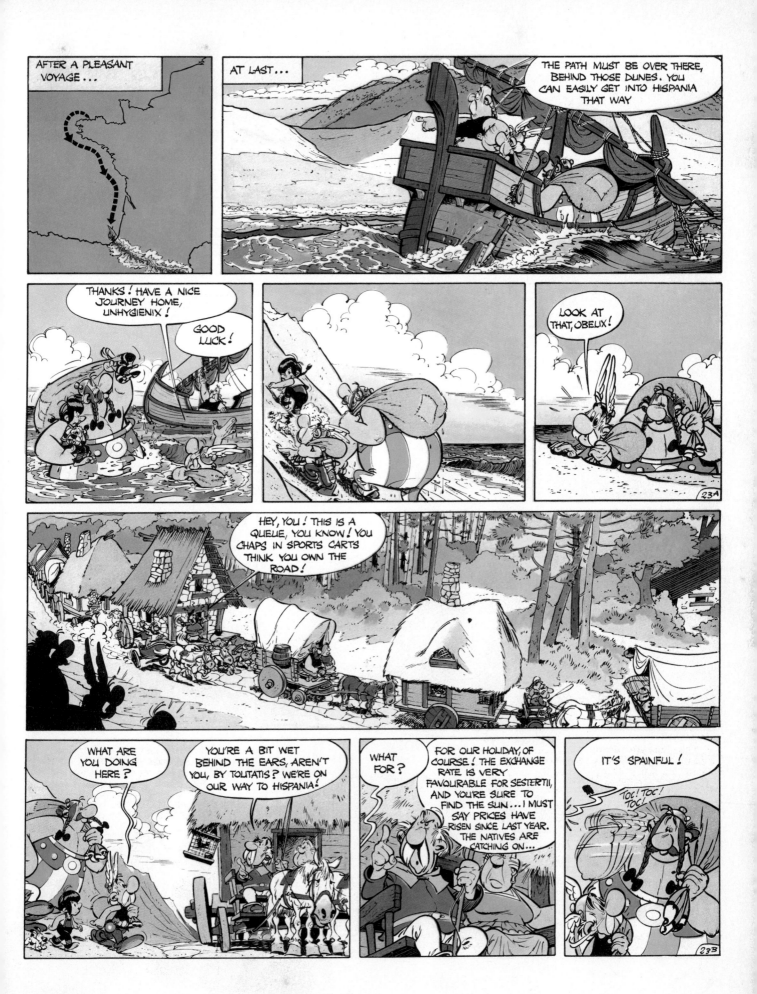

30

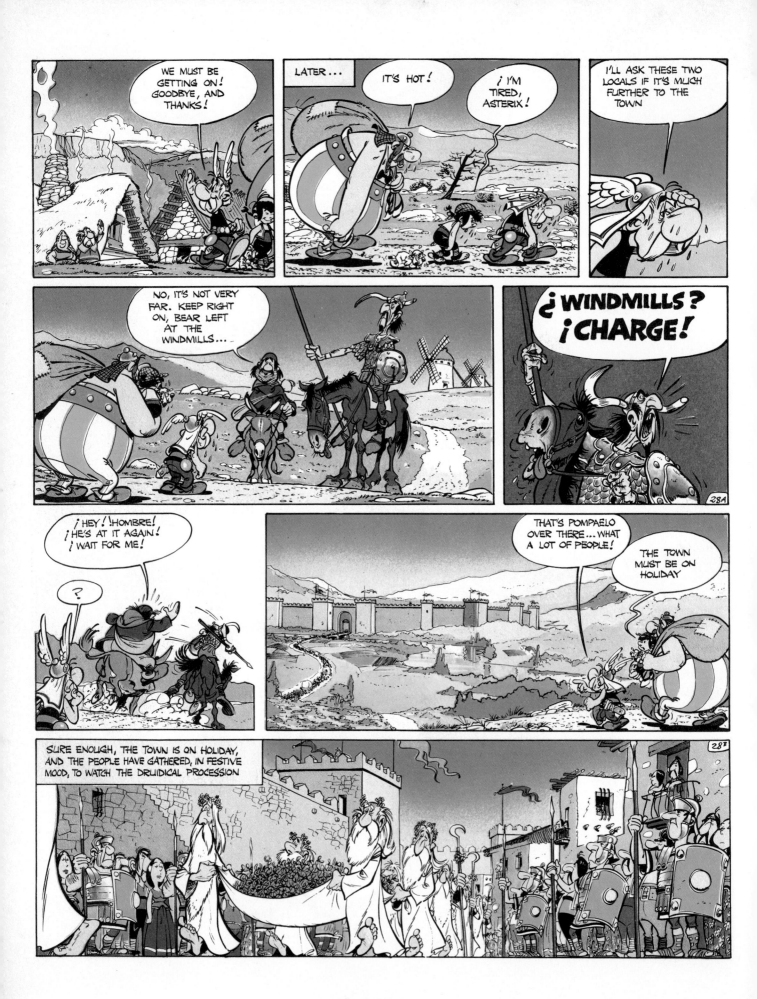

32

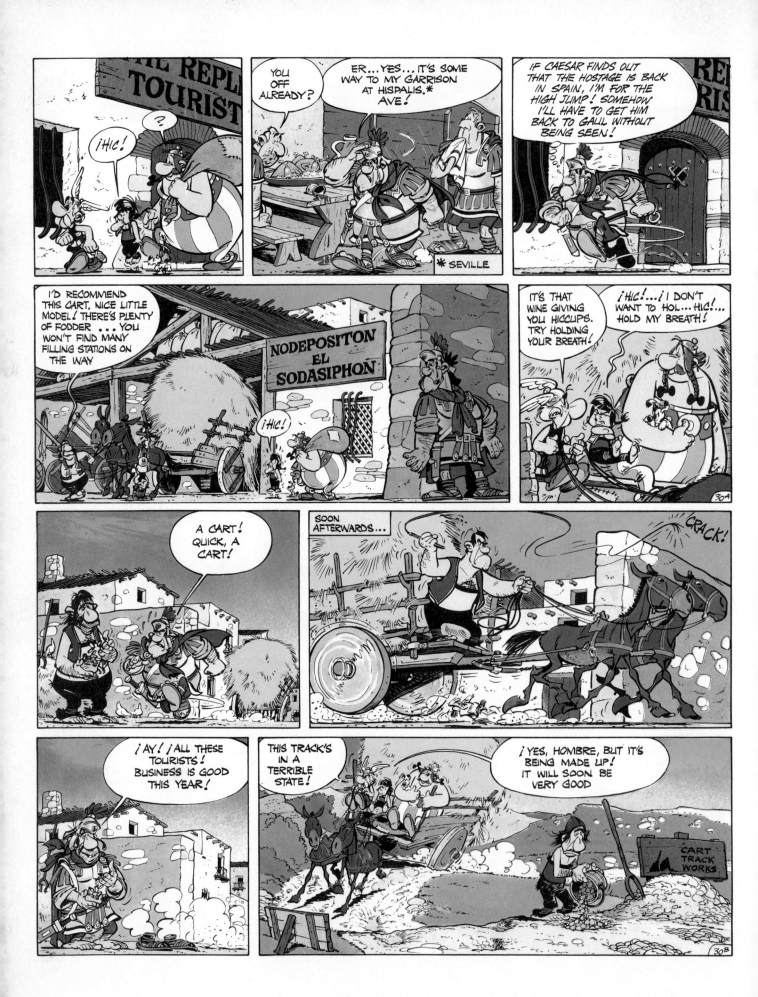

35

37

39

40

NIGHT HAS ALREADY FALLEN WHEN OUR FRIENDS ARRIVE IN HISPALIS, THE CAPITAL OF VANDALUSIA. THE MAGNIFICENT CITY IS FULL OF GAIETY. IT IS A HOLIDAY!

YOU'RE IN LUCK; I'VE GOT TWO ROOMS LEFT, NEXT DOOR TO EACH OTHER

I'M GOING TO SLEEP IN DOGMATIX'S ROOM

ME TOO!

ALL RIGHT, THEN, WE'LL SHARE THE OTHER ONE

SPLENDID! SPLENDID BY JUPI... BY OLÉ!

DINNER IN THIS TYPICAL VANDALUSIAN INN IS A CHEERFUL OCCASION

The roads are improving, They're working on them!

A proud and haughty race!

Thin-skinned!

Attractive prices, but they're rising

They've cottoned on!

The cooking's much better these day's

TODAY'S MENU IS SAUSAGE, SAUERKRAUT AND BEER

LET'S GO TO BED... WE SAY GOODBYE TOMORROW, MY DEAR AMONTILLADO EL AMOROSO!

OLOROSO EL FIASCO

GOOD NIGHT

GOOD NIGHT

NOW FOR THE MAGIC POTION! THEN I'LL BE THE STRONGEST, AND I CAN GET HOLD OF PEPE AND TAKE HIM BACK TO GAUL

ZZZZ

42

45

46